Lily of the Field

FRANCES HARIG

iUniverse, Inc.
New York   Bloomington

Lily of the Field

This is a work of fiction. All of the characters, names, incidents, organizations, and dialogue in this novel are either the products of the author's imagination or are used fictitiously.

iUniverse books may be ordered through booksellers or by contacting:

iUniverse
1663 Liberty Drive
Bloomington, IN 47403
www.iuniverse.com
1-800-Authors (1-800-288-4677)

ISBN: 978-1-4401-9649-2 (pbk)
ISBN: 978-1-4401-9650-8 (ebk)

Printed in the United States of America

iUniverse rev. date: 12/9/2009

Dedication:

I DEDICATE THIS BOOK to my Lord and Savior, Jesus Christ. To my husband, who has given me courage to publish. Also, to our five children, their spouses, nineteen grandchildren, and ten great grandchildren who give me countless joy and love.

CHAPTER 1
GHOSTS

"Why are you asking me if I believe in ghosts, Penny?" Paul asked as he narrowed his hazel eyes. He halted as he brushed back his mop of straw-colored hair. "Of course I don't believe in ghosts. You don't believe in them, do you?"

"No, I don't. It's our neighbor, that new girl in school, Ula. She told me she saw something last night and said she thought it was a ghost," Penny replied. She kicked the gravel on the road with her worn leather shoe and continued. "Ula said she saw something white drift along the fence row last night as she walked from the barn. It sort of floated near the woods and then disappeared." Penny smoothed her dress and looked at her younger brother for an answer.

"Poof, gone in an instant, huh?" he asked.

"No! Ula, said she heard a 'Whooo, whooo.' She hid behind a tree trunk and peeked around it toward the woods. It was almost dark before she spied the eerie thing. She said it was like a blob drifting around the plowed field, and then it moved into the pine trees."

"She was just trying to scare you, Penny." Paul picked up a stone and threw it as hard as he could down the road before he continued. "She gives me the creeps. Ula is thirteen years old. She's as tall as our teacher. And her black eyes have an evil look in them. She enjoys pulling and twisting the younger kids' arms before any of us see her and make her stop."

"Yes, I think she is cruel too, Paul. I'm afraid of her. Our neighbor Mrs. Johnson says that Ula's family is having a hard time just buying groceries. Her father got a job as a tenant farmer with the Kelly farms in the next county. That is why Ula is helping her family by working for the Johnsons. Anyway, she said she saw something in the field and it frightened her. Her lips trembled and her eyes looked wild when she told me. She wasn't acting so brave today. She looked scared."

"Not having enough money is no reason to be so hateful." Paul replied. "Ula is a bully; she shouldn't hurt the little ones, and I think she's lying." He picked up another stone and threw it down the road. "Mom and Dad say there are no such things as ghosts. I'd only believe it if I saw it myself, and maybe not then either. Hey, we're almost home. I'll race you to the back door." Paul took off running. "I'll beat you," he yelled.

Mother glanced out the kitchen window and watched her youngsters run up the dirt drive. She wiped her hands on her apron as Paul burst through the screen door with Penny close behind him.

"Land sakes," Mom said, "what's your hurry? Both of you act like you've seen a ghost."

"Oh, a real funny joke, Mom." Paul laughed as he hung his red sweatshirt and hat on a peg. "I won, I'm the greatest winner, Penny!" Paul bragged.

"Just because you got a head start is all," Penny defended as she hung her blue sweater next to his.

Paul turned to Mom. "Just wait till Penny tells you the

lie Ula told her. I *should say Ooo-la*. Even her name sounds spooky. Boy! I am hungry. May we have a snack?"

Penny said, "I'm hungry too, Mom. Ula told me she saw a ghost last night over in the Johnsons' field behind their barn. The moon was full and cast a soft light, so she could see something appearing and disappearing."

Mother smiled, and her green eyes with brown dots, like Paul's, crinkled at the corners. She gave a soft sigh and eased her slight frame on a wooden chair at the kitchen table. "Whew! I've had a busy day," she commented. "I want to hear all about it, but first Penny, get a pitcher of milk from the basement, and Paul, get the tin of peanut butter cookies from the cupboard." As she poured the milk, Mother said, "Now then, what's all this about Ula? Is she causing more trouble in school by trying to scare the children?"

Penny dunked her cookie in a glass of milk and related the story. "You know, Mom, she was hired by the Johnsons to help on their farm this summer. All the kids at school say she looks like a gypsy. Her black hair reaches to her waist and she wears long, bright skirts and earrings."

"Yes, Penny. Sara told me Ula's parents came from Europe when she was just a small child. Her family has moved often." Mother patted the knot of light brown hair on the back of her neck and gave a thoughtful frown. "Some children are taught all sorts of strange and superstitious tales. Maybe that's why Ula thinks she saw a ghost."

Paul interrupted while stuffing a cookie in his mouth. "Naw, she's just crazy."

"Don't call her names and don't talk with your mouth full," Mother scolded. "I'm sure what she saw wasn't anything unnatural. She might tell a scary story to get people to notice her.

She probably causes trouble for the same reason, but it's not right for her to act that way. Now you scoot upstairs and change your clothes. It's time to do your chores. Paul, gather the eggs and get the news paper from the mailbox. Penny, peel potatoes for supper. Dad will be starved by the time he comes in from working the field."

While the two were changing, Paul called to Penny. "Mom doesn't know what Ula is like. It's worse than trying to get attention from us. She told one of the little girls, Mary, she was going to put a curse on her. Mary started to cry and Ula laughed at her."

"I know, Paul, she acts like she has some power she can call on to harm us. She is creepy. No one wants to get on her bad side. Mrs. Miller never hears Ula telling all her weird stories and saying she wants us to be hurt or punished. She is so scary. She'd have friends if she was nice to us."

"Dad will be here soon. We need to tell Mom and him what's going on. They will probably know what to do about her." Paul shared.

"Of course you're right, Paul" Penny answered. "I don't like to tattle, and it would make Ula even worse if she thought we told on her. We must ask Dad and Mom not to tell on us, but they should know how she bosses all of the kids at school. She acts so sweet and nice to Mrs. Miller, our teacher."

CHAPTER 2
DAD'S STORY

"Yum, something smells good!" Dad grinned and pulled off his work boots and began to roll up the sleeves of his shirt. "Work outside makes me so hungry I could eat a skunk."

Mom smiled. "Maybe someday I'll just feed you one instead of preparing a home-cooked meal."

Dad's brown eyes twinkled as he pumped water and filled the wash basin in the sink. He rinsed his face and soaped his hands and muscular arms. "Ooh, I think I might possibly be able to tell the difference," he teased. "Let's see what news is in the paper tonight. I can't believe we are in the fourth month of 1948 already. It seems as if the New Year just started. Well, nothing exciting reported today. Come on, kids. Supper's ready. Let's pray."

While the Lloyd Harris family bowed their heads, animals from the fields and forest cautiously crept toward the family pond to quench their thirst. The creatures paid little attention to the faded white farmhouse nestled on a gentle hill above the water. The windows sent soft rays of light shimmering onto the pool.

Dad chuckled as he moved across the kitchen to get another cup of coffee. He brushed a wisp of brown hair away from his face and turned to Penny. "So, Ula is scaring the kids with her story? Well, there're all sorts of mysterious tales in the world. In my life I've found all stories have an explanation, honey. You and Paul sit at the table, and I'll tell you about one of those. This is the truth and it happened to me."

"Yeah, yeah! Tell us your story." Paul begged.

"Well, I was ten years old. Just about your age, Paul. My brothers and I made a makeshift trapeze to play on at the river near our home. A huge maple grew on the bank, and its branches hung out over the river. We found a length of rope in our shed and dragged it to our hangout.

"I was elected to shimmy up the giant tree and inch across the limb draped over the water. I scooted out far enough, hugged the rough branch, and tucked my feet around the bottom. My job was to tie the rope around the limb. The problem happened to be my arms weren't long enough.

"After some thought I swung the rope down under the limb until it whipped up the other side and wrapped around the branch. I tied it tight and tossed the remainder to my brothers.

"Eddy was eight, thin, and tall like me. Roy was almost six. We called him a baby. He was chubby and kind of short. We hefted Roy to a low crotch, and he tucked the rope in place, and then it was set up.

"Whenever we could, we'd hurry to the river. I'd grab the line, run as fast as I could, plant my feet on the end of the knot, and sail over the water. I felt like a bird soaring above the earth. I'd loosen my grip and plunge into the river.

"We played after our work was done during the summer and had a super time. It was such fun. In the fall after school started, we decided to stop and play one more time. Which was strictly against our mother's orders because the weather had turned too cold.. I had a heavy coat bundled around me. I grabbed the rope, dashed as fast as I could, and flew over the river. I reached a lofty height, and before I started to swing down, the rope broke.

"My body hit the river like a rock. Thousands of icicles clutched at my skin and fought to drag me under the surface. I felt myself sinking. Eddy screamed from the bank, 'Keep swimming!'

"Fear prickled my mind. 'Help, help,' I cried. I thought I was going to die! A log floated in front of me and I felt a pressure on my waist. My body was pushed next to the log. I grabbed it and floated to shore.

"Eddy yelled to Roy, 'I hear a car coming. Run up the bank and wave it down. We need help.' Roy was staring my way and didn't move. Eddy shouted at Roy again, more intense this time. Roy jumped and ran.

"Our neighbor, Ol' Henry, stopped his jalopy and scolded us all the while he helped us. 'What in tarnation are you doin'? Trying to kill each other? Ed and Roy, you two skedaddle to school. I'll take care of your brother Lloyd.' Henry grabbed a small tree trunk and pulled me up the bank to his car.

CHAPTER 3

HEAVENLY BEING

"I don't ever remember being so frightened," continued Dad soberly. "I was frozen inside and out and shaking like a leaf on a windy day.

"One minute Mom would scold me because I disobeyed. The next minute she'd cry and hug me, grateful I was alive. She stripped me of my wet clothes and wrapped sheet blankets and quilts around me. My body still shivered like a leaf in a wind storm. We didn't have electricity in those days. Mom heated water on our stove and put the hot water in jars, like she was canning. Next, she folded each of the jars in a towel so she wouldn't burn me, and she placed them around my body. Slowly the heat began to penetrate, and soon I fell into a deep sleep."

Penny's face flushed. She got up from her chair and gave Dad a hug. "I'm glad you're here, Dad," she said, her eyes moist.

"I'm glad you're here, too," Paul urged. "So you can finish your story."

"Well, the next day my folks were sure I was back to normal. So, off to the wood shed I went. My Dad gave me three whacks on my rump. With each swat my tears flowed faster. I knew I was guilty. Dad waited until I calmed. He took me in his arms and gave me a hug.

"'Listen, son.' His voice caught. 'Don't ever do a stupid stunt and not obey us again. You could have drowned. We would have lost you.'

"It was hard for me to talk. My throat was tight, but I had to tell Dad someone or something lifted me onto the log. 'I can't explain it,' I told him, 'but I know I felt a hand on my back, and I was pushed onto the log.'

"Dad was bewildered. He was a powerful man of medium height, stocky and strong. He could handle almost anything, but this stumped him.

"'Little Roy told us he saw a person in the river. I didn't believe him. He said a tall, handsome man waved at him. As the man smiled, he lifted you on the log with his other hand. Now, I know the water is at least six feet deep there. For someone to stand in it, he'd have to be unnaturally tall.' Dad shook his head. 'Unless … it's hardly believable, but the only explanation is an angel.'"

"Not a real angel." Penny gasped.

Dad nodded his head. "In the book of Hebrews, it says many have entertained angels unawares. It seems we are some of the few who are aware!"

Penny clapped her hands. "I love your story."

Paul bolted from his chair and jumped around the kitchen "Angels, mysteries, and spooks floating in the field. It's so exciting around our place!"

"Settle down, Paul," Mother fussed, "and sit yourself at the table for dessert." She set a baking pan on the cupboard and cut generous pieces of yellow cake covered with thick chocolate frosting.

"Remember what I told you, kids," Dad added, "this isn't just a story; it really happened to me."

CHAPTER 4
THE SIGHTING

"Wow!" Penny said. "Just think of it a visitor from heaven here on the earth."

Mom served a piece of cake to Dad and pointed. "Take a look outside. The sunset is beautiful. If I could paint, I'd have a scene like this one hung in the living room. See how many pretty colors there are."

Penny began to count, "Red, blue, yellow, purple… Wait a minute. Look! There's something moving on the far side of the pond. I'll press my face close to the window and see if I can tell what it is. It's not clear. It's too dark outside to identify it. Whatever it is, it's white. Now it disappeared! Wait … there it is again."

"It is white," Paul said. "It's too big to be a cat. Hey, maybe it's Grandma's dog, Prince."

"Here, scoot over and let me see," Dad said. He wiped the steamed pane with his sleeve and strained to see the object. "If it's Grandma's white German shepherd we'll be able to call him. Still, it seems to hop, and it doesn't move like old Prince."

Dad opened the door and whistled, "Come 'ere, Prince, come ' ere, old fella."

Nothing came or answered his call. Whatever they had seen was no longer visible.

Penny turned to Paul. "What do you think it is, Paul?"

"Maybe it's Ula's spook. It floats by the swamp," he teased.

"Well," answered Dad, "whatever it is we saw lives and moves. It's too dark out to identify the shape."

"You two better get your chores done," Mom ordered. "It'll soon be bedtime. Finish your cake and help me with supper dishes, Penny. Paul, go finish your homework."

Dad added, "I'll take you out in the morning to check for tracks. Maybe we can figure out what our mysterious blob of white is."

Later, in her bed, Penny lay awake. Paul was in his room across the hall making soft "OOOeeee" noises.

"You don't scare me," she whispered as loud as she could. "You'd like everyone to think you're smarter than I am. Some people think you're as old as I am ... but never, never as smart." Penny giggled. "It's easy for people to believe you're my age. You've grown tall this year. Grandma said to me last week, 'Honestly, you look like twins with your blonde hair and freckles on your cheeks.'"

Paul whispered back, "I'm at least as tall as you and twice as smart, but I don't look like any old girl, and not like you with your yellow cat eyes."

"They're light brown. Not yellow," Penny argued.

Mother called from the bottom of the stairs, "Enough talking. Go to sleep!"

Penny smiled to herself, *As if I thought Ula actually saw a ghost and we did too. No, something alive moved around the pond. What was it, though, that eerie white shape?* Her head whirled with fairy tales as she dropped off to sleep, snug in the warmth and softness of her oak bed.

Boom! Boom! Penny opened her eyes. "Oh, no, lightning." She cowered under her covers. ***Boom!*** "Dad … Mom, are you awake?" she called. Carefully she crept out of her room.

Mother appeared at the bottom of the stairs with a kerosene lamp. "All of us are out of bed, honey. Come down and sit in the living room."

Paul hopped around the living room. "I love a wild storm," he hollered. "Our lights have blown. Wow! Penny, how could you sleep?"

Mom placed the lamp on an end table in the living room. "I think we should sit here together for a while," she warned. "April is too early in the season to have a warm day like we had today. Michigan is known for how fast, severe weather can blow across the Great Lakes."

"Look at the branches of the maple trees in our yard," Penny said and pointed. "In the lightning they look like skinny long arms reaching out for us."

"Girls," muttered Paul. "This is a great storm."

Crash! Glass flew as a limb broke a front window.

"Everyone to the basement," Dad ordered. He blew out the lamp and turned on a large battery flashlight. "It's a small room and a little musty smelling, but we'll be safe down here,"

The storm passed as quickly as it arrived and was soon only a faint rumble in the distance.

Back upstairs, Dad lit their kerosene lantern and grabbed the handle. "Come on, Paul. We need to find some boards in the woodshed to cover the broken window."

In the soft glow of the lamp Mom warned, "Penny, watch for broken glass. I don't want you to get cut. Here, hold the dustpan and I'll sweep the shattered window into it." Carefully Mother inspected the floor. "Good, it looks like we can mop up the water."

Bang. Bang. Bang. "The covered window looks secure."

Dad stepped back to view his work. "We'll be dry for tonight."

"Boy am I tired," Mom exclaimed. "I've had enough excitement for one day. Come on, you two, I'll light the way to your rooms."

CHAPTER 5
SCHOOL DAYS

THE MORNING AFTER THE storm, the sun rose to show what damage had taken place. Dad and Paul had finished the morning milking and were enjoying breakfast.

"Whew, what a powerful wind last night," Dad commented. "The towering oak on the other side of the road blew over and looks like a giant lying in the grass."

Paul answered, "I think the lightning hit close, 'cause it sure cracked loud and thundered at the same time."

Dad slid back his chair. "You're right, Son. We are fortunate that all the damage we had was a broken window." He turned to Mom and gave her a grin. "I need to go to town and get a pane of glass, honey. You kids get your books and stuff, and I'll give you a ride to school."

Penny ran to the undamaged window in the living room. "I can see the Watson kids coming. They should be here in a few minutes. Would you wait for them, Dad?"

"Sure, honey," answered Dad as he moved to the stove and poured more coffee into his cup.

Soon everyone sat in the car. Mary, the oldest, was twelve, Penny's age; Mark was one year younger than Paul, and Betty was six.

Dad drove his car full of people into the driveway of the school. A plump, dark-haired young woman approached smiling.

"Do you have any damage to the school because of the storm, Miss Miller?" Dad asked as he rolled down the window of his green Hudson.

"Nothing serious," the teacher reported. "Only a few shingles blew off on the side of the roof."

"I'll ask one of the neighbors to help me, and we'll check on the roof later today." Dad said.

"Thanks, I appreciate your help." She waved as Dad left for town.

Penny and Paul told everyone about their broken window.

Mary's long, dark braids hung to her waist as she grimly told everyone. "Our family heard tapping on the windows. Mom said it was hail. The wind blew like crazy and our old shed out back fell down. One minute we could see it in the lightning, and in the next flash it was gone."

Bruce Anderson nodded his dark eyes shown under his blue denim cap. "We had a barn door blow right off its rail. It seems as if the storm hit every family around us."

"Our family had even more excitement earlier," Paul said. "We saw something white float by our pond in the field. It was almost dark and we couldn't see it clearly. It would appear and disappear."

Ula stood nearby. Her dark eyes flashing. "What did you see, Paul?" She demanded as she grabbed his arm and began to twist. Did you see an evil spirit? Tell me now!"

Paul fought and tried to pull away.

"Let go of my brother!" Penny yelled, and shoved Ula.

"Oh, so your baby brother can't take care of himself, huh? I'll just have to get it out of you instead, Penny," Ula threatened as she ran after Penny.

"Quit being a bully," Paul shouted.

Miss Miller, unaware of the fight, grabbed the thick bell rope in the hall of the school and pulled. "Clang, clang," the message rang out for school to start.

"I'll get you later," Ula sneered. "You saw a spirit. It'll give all of you bad luck. I'll see it does for sure. I'll put a spell on you."

Penny jerked free and ran through the school door. She threw her sweater on a bench.

"Stay away from me, Ula," she warned. "Just because you're bigger, you think you can boss me around. And there isn't any old evil spirit, either." Penny yelled over her shoulder.

The children filed into the one room school and found their seats in the four rows of desks.

Penny's face was red with anger as she repeated the Pledge of Allegiance, but she softened as she sang "God Bless America."

"Everyone may be seated now." Miss Miller said. "If you have any school work to do you have some time to finish it."

She smoothed her hair on the way to her desk. At the front of the room, she busied herself with the lessons of the day.

Penny lifted the top of the wooden desk and checked her arithmetic paper. "Three more problems to solve," she groaned quietly. "I forgot to put the date on the upper right hand side of my paper. It's April 10, 1948. Good, I'm almost done."

Soon Miss Miller called the seventh grade to the big table at the right of the desks.

Mary, Bruce, and Penny exchanged papers, and corrected each other's math problems as Miss Miller gave the answers.

"These long division problems take forever," Penny moaned as they were given their new assignment.

Her teacher agreed. "Remember, it helps to know your multiplication tables. You all did well today. If any of you has trouble, raise your hand and I'll help you. You may return to your desks."

CHAPTER 6
THE LONG DAY

PENNY'S THOUGHTS TURNED TO Ula's threats. *She thinks we saw a spirit, but it wasn't a ghost or a spirit. It is just some sort of animal.* Penny gave a deep sigh. *I'd better work on these problems or I'll never get them done.*

Each of the grades took its turn at the big desk until recess.

Penny, Mary, and Kate met under the apple tree behind school.

"Boy, I am glad Miss Miller is keeping Ula in again," Kate said as she brushed a twig away from her auburn ringlets.

Mary took a bite of her juicy apple. "I think she has her stay in because she knows Ula picks on us."

Penny took a sugar cookie from wax paper and took a bite. Her blonde hair ruffled in the breeze. "Yeah, you're right, Mary. Even so, I think Miss Miller does want to teach Ula, if Ula will listen to her."

"Ula likes her a lot. You can see how she obeys her," Kate said. "She's always respectful to Miss Miller."

Penny closed her lunch box. "She doesn't care what she does to us kids, though."

The girls nodded in agreement.

"Let's climb on these low branches," Mary suggested, as she grabbed a limb, swung and sat on a branch. "What do you think you saw last night, all scary and white?" she asked.

Penny rested in a crotch near Mary and squinted to keep the sun out of her eyes. "It wasn't spooky. Well, maybe a little. Dad said it has to be some sort of animal. He was going to take us out this morning to look for tracks, but the rain washed away all the clues.

Paul and Mark raced across the grass toward the girls.

"What do you think you saw last night, Paul?" Kate asked. Kate's chestnut colored hair shown like a crown in the sun. It brought out her freckles and blue eyes.

Paul glanced at Kate and his face turned light pink. "Well, uh," he stammered, "I don't know. I've been thinking." He took his shirttail and wiped his forehead. "It was about the size of a goat and it kind of jerked or jumped," Paul mumbled. "It reminded me of a goat."

"A goat!" Mark said, "Naw! Nobody's got goats around here."

"Yeah, I know," Paul agreed. "I'm just telling you what it looked like to me."

The bell broke their conversation, and the sixteen students filed to their desks.

Miss Miller smiled gently at her students and thought, *I certainly can't blame the children for being so restless. We must have spring fever. They'll be happy when it's time to dismiss them.*

With such beautiful sunshine outside, the day seemed to drag along like a snail on a long journey.

"Finally, school is over until Monday." Mary sighed. "My chore for this week is dusting. It's my favorite job. I like to make everything shine."

Penny approached the large green chalkboard at the front of the room. She turned to Betty, who was waiting for her sister. "Want to help me clean erasers outside?"

"Sure." Betty jumped and followed Penny to the cement steps in front of the school.

"See Betty, if you hit the erasers together, little puffy clouds of chalk drift in the air."

Betty laughed in delight and smacked the erasers until no dust was left.

"The chalk almost looks like what we saw last night, a white cloud in the field. Okay, we're done now. Let's find Mary, Mark, and Paul."

"I wonder if we'll see our mysterious white object in the cornfield today," Penny wondered out loud as the small band neared the Harris farm.

"We don't want to see anything weird, day or night," Mary said. "It's supposed to be an animal, right? It wouldn't be here now. Would it? You said you saw the white thing when it was almost dark."

"You're right, Mary. It's the wrong time of day to find anything. Here's our field," Paul pointed. "Mark and I will check it out. Whatever the blob was probably crossed the road right about here."

"Come on everyone. Let's get out of here—run!" Beth motioned and dashed away.

Penny and Mary followed Beth, and left the boys to look for their "ghost." "Our brothers sure know how to scare us. Look, they're laughing," Mary said.

"Here's my house. I feel safe now," Penny giggled.

Paul and Mark quickly caught up with the girls. "There isn't anything in the field," Mark reported.

"Keep looking for your white spook," Mark yelled to Paul. "We'll see you in church Sunday. You can tell us if you've seen it again and what you've found."

"Sure thing," Paul waved.

CHAPTER 7
ULA

ULA WAITED BY THE Johnsons' screen door and looked outside often. "My folks will be here any minute," she said.

"You miss your family a lot, don't you, Ula?" Sarah Johnson asked. "This is the first time you've been away from them for so long."

"Yes, it is. You know I'm the oldest and I need to help my family by working for you." Ula proudly held her pay. She kept it in a colorful cloth purse her mother had given her before she left home. "Look! Here they come." She pushed open the screen door and ran to the lawn.

The old car trailed a cloud of dust and blue smoke behind it. All four doors burst open and Ula's two brothers and three sisters piled out of the auto. Everyone yelled, "Ula!" Arms outstretched, they laughed, cried, hugged, and danced around the yard.

Ula's father clapped his hands. "Get in the car." He smiled

and showed even, white teeth. He cranked the engine, it back-fired, and they drove away in a hurry.

"Good-bye, see you Sunday." Ula waved to Mrs. Johnson, who stood on the porch stairs.

"I've missed all of you so much. It's been a whole month since I've been home," Ula said.

"We've missed you lots too," Mom answered. "How is work? Do you like Mrs. Johnson? How is school? I need to know all about everything."

"Well, Mom, Mrs. Johnson is nice. Work is okay, not very hard. But the kids at school make fun of me. I hate them. I'm older and bigger than most of them except for a couple of the boys. Miss Miller is teaching me fourth grade lessons during recess. She says she thinks I'm behind because we've moved a lot and I've missed so many lessons. But she also says I'm smart. I'm learning fast and I'll catch up soon."

"You've always been smart and strong," Mom answered and gave Ula a big hug.

"Guess what I saw at the Johnson farm?" Ula asked.

"Well, what? I just can't guess," Mom answered.

"I think it was a spirit. It was white and it would disap-pear right before my eyes. I saw it at night in the field. What do you think?"

"It might be a spirit," Dad said. "Were you close enough to call to it? Did it look at you?"

"No, I stood on the other side of the field. I watched it for about five minutes. It went into the woods and I haven't seen it since."

"We'll ask the tea leaves tonight," Mother said. "They'll tell us about it."

After supper the family sat outside around a campfire. Dad played his fiddle. A tear slid down Ula's cheek. "I love our music," Ula cried. "Do I have to leave and go back to work?"

"I'm sorry." Mother folded her arms around Ula. "We need

the money. Your brothers and sisters need clothes, shoes and food. Maybe we'll have a good harvest this fall and you can move back home."

"I hope so," Ula said. "There are a couple of kids at school the rest of the kids all like. I think it's those two who tell the others to tease me. The girl's name is Penny and her brother, Paul. Show me how to put a spell on them. Penny fights with me. She thinks she's so smart."

"It's sleepy time for the little ones," said Mother. "Help me to put them to bed and now we'll ask the tea leaves. They'll show you what to do with Penny and Paul, and with the white spirit."

CHAPTER 8
SUNDAY

I LIKE SUNDAY MORNING. I can sleep in a little bit. Penny thought and looked around. *I like my room. It's large enough for my bed and dresser. Mom let me put pictures from last year's calendar on my walls. I like the landscapes and ocean scenes, but the animal pictures are the best. The deer are the prettiest of all. Their eyes are so soft and big. Mom says they are like the ballet dancers of the woods.*

"Penny," Mom called. "It's time to get ready for church."

"Okay Mom, I'll be down as soon as I get my Sunday dress from the closet."

After breakfast, everyone was ready. Dad straightened his tie and Mother checked to see if her hat looked straight.

"Wouldn't it be nice if we had our own building to hold church in and a regular minister?" Mother asked.

"You bet," Dad agreed. "Even so, we're blessed to have a large wood building to meet in. We hold all sorts of meetings and social events in the Grange Hall. Come on everybody, find a seat in the car. We don't want to be late!"

A small circle of chairs was arranged for Penny's class and she quickly found a seat.

"Hi, Mrs. O'Brien," Penny greeted. "I've got something exciting to share today."

"Good. I think I know a little about your adventure. We're all anxious to hear more about it from you," replied her teacher, who was also Kate's mother. "First let's have a word of prayer."

She bowed her auburn hair and closed her blue eyes.

Kate and her mom look so much alike, Penny observed before closing her own eyes.

Mrs. O'Brien straightened the white collar on her navy suit and began, "Father, bless our class and our lesson. Guide each of us to learn a new truth from your word today. Amen."

Penny raised her hand and shared in an excited voice the Thursday night sighting, and how the mysterious object faded away. "And we haven't seen it since," she ended.

Mrs. O'Brien was pleased. "Your experience goes right along with today's lesson. Jesus' disciples were on a large lake. Their destination was Gennesaret. It was around three o'clock in the morning, dark and windy. The waves were high and they had trouble rowing to shore. Jesus had stayed on land the evening before and told them he would meet them later. In the dark, some of the disciples saw a form move toward them on the water. It wasn't another boat and it didn't make any noise. They screamed in terror."

"Think about this," Mrs. O'Brien challenged the class. "First: It was late at night. Second: The wind tossed the boat in different directions. Third: A figure walked toward them on the water. They thought it was a ghost. Do you know what it was, class?"

"I don't know, but it sure sounds spooky. I'd probably

think it was some kind of sea monster." Sally's head shook with mock fright.

Paul raised his hand. "It was Jesus walking on the water."

"Correct," their teacher nodded.

Penny added, "Peter jumped out of the boat and walked on the water toward Jesus."

"Right!" exclaimed Mrs. O'Brien. "Who knows what happened to Peter?"

No one answered. "Let's check our story again," their teacher instructed.

She took her black leather Bible and read the account. "Why did Peter start to sink?"

Penny raised her hand. "My scripture says Peter became afraid of the huge waves around him. He took his eyes off Jesus and started to sink. Jesus took hold of Peter's hand and they walked to the boat."

"Exactly," Mrs. O'Brien replied. "Does anyone of you think this story might apply to what Penny and Paul's family saw last night?"

"They didn't see a person walking on the water," Sally offered.

"It wasn't a ghost either. There's no such thing as ghosts," Kate replied.

"You're right," Mrs. O'Brien stated and continued. "But these things are similar. The Harris family didn't know what they saw. They said it looked like a ghost. The sky was dark. I think we should pray, and keep our eyes on Jesus. We'll ask Him to show Penny and Paul what they saw. Jesus can walk on the water and He knows all mysteries."

"We had a neat lesson in Sunday school today," Penny shared on the way home. "Mrs. O'Brien says the Bible teaches there isn't anything on this earth or in the heavens that God has not made. So what we saw in the field has to be something from Him and He will show us what it is."

"I couldn't have any better answer," Dad said. "Here we are at home. Boy! I'm so hungry my backbone is hitting my belly."

"Me too," Paul groaned and held his stomach.

Mother laughed. "I know, I know. Lunch will be ready soon. I'll heat the leftover vegetable soup. Penny, set the table and we'll feed our starved men."

"No one can make soup as lip-smackin good as you can. It tastes more-ish. It makes me want more," Dad nodded to Mom. "It's probably your homemade bread that enriches the flavor."

"You and your food," Mom said and leaned over and gave Dad a kiss on his cheek.

"Your food hits the spot," Dad complimented, after he had eaten two large bowls of soup and gave a yawn. "I think I'll take a nap."

"May we go to the big woods, Dad?" Paul asked.

"Sure, just be careful."

"We'll let you know when we want you back. We'll blow the car horn three times," Mother told them.

"Hurry, Penny," Paul yelled upstairs.

"I'll be down in a minute. I need to change into my old clothes," Penny answered.

Paul grabbed his favorite red sweatshirt. It was worn and faded, but it he prized it. Soon the two were on their way.

"Yesterday I scared a rabbit out of hiding next to the barn." Paul shared. "Let's take the cow path to the woods, Penny. Do you think we'll see our floating white thing?"

"We can look, but if it's something dangerous or spooky I'm not standing around," Penny promised.

CHAPTER 9
DANGEROUS ENCOUNTER

"Let's look for frogs next to the creek." Paul suggested.

Kerplunk, a frog hit the water and fled from the two hunters.

Paul lay on the bank and peeked over the edge. "Hey, talk about walking on the water. Come here and see the water spiders, Penny."

"Sure enough," Penny said and looked over the bank. "Just look at them. They're like miniature skaters. God made it easy for them to skim across the surface, but impossible for us."

"Come on, let's find a big tree to climb," Paul yelled and ran ahead.

"Here's a tall one. Oof," Paul grunted and pulled his body to a leafy branch. "Give me your hand, Penny, and I'll help you up next to me. We'll be camouflaged so nothing can see us."

Penny watched for any movement in the woods. A chipmunk ran near the trunk of their tree. It stopped, sat on its hind legs, and munched some seeds.

"Its cheeks are full of food to take to its nest. He's *so* cute," Penny observed.

"Shhh! We won't see anything with you talking." Paul warned.

Penny sat still and whispered. "I'm not so sure I want to find out what the white thing is we saw." After a short time she turned and said, "I don't know why, Paul, but I feel scared. I want to start back home," she whispered.

"Shhh," Paul warned again. "Listen, I hear something."

Penny sat still. Her eyes held fear. "Do you hear a voice?" she asked. Her heart pounded. "Oh no, look! It's Ula!"

Paul quickly climbed farther up the tree.

"Oh, white spirit of the forest, appear to me," Ula sang. In rhythm to the tune she swung her body back and forth. All at once she stopped directly under the tree Penny and Paul had climbed.

Beep, beep, beep. The Harris car horn blew.

Penny jerked at the sound, lost her balance, fell, and landed at Ula's feet.

Ula stepped backward. "What are you doing? Are you spying on me? Why are you in my woods?" Ula sneered. "What were you doing in my tree?"

Penny's fear quickly changed to anger. "What do you mean *your* tree? This is our woods and our tree. You are trespassing! Get off my property, Ula!"

Ula grabbed Penny's arm and started to twist. "You're not telling me what I can and can't do, little girl," she ordered. "I'll teach you a lesson," Ula threatened.

Paul tumbled from the tree and walked in front of Ula.

"Do you know what you need, Ula?" Paul asked softly.

Ula loosened her grip on Penny and turned to Paul. "Where did you come from, Paul? No, I don't need nothin'."

Paul took a step closer and stared into her face. "Yes you do, Ula. God loves you and so does Jesus. Jesus is waiting for you to love Him back."

Beep, Beep, Beep.

"Dad and Mom are signaling for us to go home with the car horn, Ula. Remember what I said."

Paul turned slowly and walked away. "Come on, Penny. Let's go … fast," he spoke in a whisper.

Penny had been rooted to the spot. Shaken, she moved, followed her brother, and glanced back. Ula stood in the same place and stared after them as though Paul had slapped her face.

CHAPTER 10
MYSTERY SOLVED

A HUGE RED ROOSTER crowed loudly and tried to perch on Penny's arm. Slowly she opened her eyes and became aware the rooster was in her dream. His crowing was real, because Rowdy made his presence known all over the farm. She squinted to sunlight streaming through sheer white curtains. At once the excitement from the night before returned. She threw off her warm quilt and ran down the stairs.

It had been almost two weeks since they saw the strange white blob down by the pond. Last night all of them had briefly seen it gently move around the north field. It was still too dark to identify what it was. The shape appeared and disappeared.

Penny planted a kiss on her mother's cheek. "Good morning, Mom," she sang. "Is Dad ready to take us on our trip to see if we can find out what our ghost really is?"

"Whoopee!" Paul stomped down the stairs before she finished.

Mother laughed and said, "You two better have some breakfast and get washed and dressed first. Dad should be in from the barn soon."

"Mmm, these pancakes are good," Paul said as he stacked a pile on his plate. "Maple syrup makes them taste '**more-ish**.'"

"Sure does." replied Penny. "Maybe Dad was eating pancakes when he invented that word." Penny finished and excused herself from the table.

"Hurry, Paul, I'm going to make my bed and get ready."

He nodded to her, his mouth too full of pancakes to answer.

In a short while Mother called, "Here comes your dad. You better get your boots on. It's muddy in the field."

The sun shone warm on their faces and the killdeer sang a shrill song. They left footprints as they trudged to the spot they were about to search. It was mushy between the rows of corn stubble.

Penny spotted bird and raccoon tracks in the soft brown earth. "I don't see anything unusual," she said.

Paul hollered. "Come over here." He motioned and pointed at the ground.

"Yep, a deer track," Dad identified. "Look next to it. What do you see?"

Penny and Paul shook their heads. "All we see are some holes about the size of a quarter."

"Do you know what they are, Dad?" Penny asked.

"Well, I'll be!" Dad exclaimed with a wide grin on his face. "All we could see last night was a whitish form, right?" Dads' eyes twinkled. "We couldn't see this doe, because her coat blended with the brown of the field. These marks next to hers are a fawn's."

"No, I don't think so, Dad," Penny argued. "A fawn would blend in too. They have some white spots, but not enough to see what we did. The animal was all white and would disappear right before our eyes."

Dad smiled. "Not this one, honey. Our mysterious animal has to be a rare albino fawn."

"Ooh!" Penny and Paul said together. "Just think—a snow white fawn!"

Paul became serious. "How can a little deer all white be protected, Dad? You'd think it wouldn't be able to hide like the others."

Dad answered, "When a fawn lies down it disappears in the grass. Even a grown deer is hard to spot in the woods. Soon the wild white lilies called trillium will bloom. Maybe its mother will hide it among the flowers. God gives animals a natural instinct to protect themselves."

Penny could imagine the doe nudging her baby to a patch of lilies. The soft yellow and pinks of the surrounding brush would camouflage the fawn. The leaves and three petals of the lilies would look like a carpet of green and white covering the ground. The fawn's ears would look like the tips of the lily petals.

Dad broke the silence. "It must be at least a month old. It doesn't take long for a fawn to be able to run next to its mother like this one does. I can see why it would disappear. The doe is the color of our field. She would blend in with the brown dirt so we couldn't see her. When the little fawn moved to the other side of her mother, it seemed to disappear."

Penny's eyes shone with excitement. "Let's tame it, Paul. We can wait until we see it again and make it our pet!"

"Good idea. We'll do it!" Paul answered excitedly.

"Wait a minute you two," Dad said "Chances are you'll never see it again. Don't get your hopes up about taming a wild animal. They're about impossible to get close to. Even if you did see it again, the doe would sense danger and run away to keep her baby safe. Let's go home and tell Mom the news. Won't she be surprised?"

CHAPTER 11

THE FAWN HUNT

"Yippee! Finally it's the end of May. I'm glad school is out," Paul ran next to Penny. "We'll have time to find our albino fawn."

"Yes, we'll have all summer," Penny answered. "I've thought about it too. Dad told us to search for a deer trail in the woods. We could make a deer blind in a tree close to the trail. Maybe the fawn will follow its mother and we'll be able to tame them both."

"Remember, Dad doesn't think we can get close, but your plan sounds great. We'll start as soon as we get home," Paul said.

"We'll have to do our chores first. I'm sure Mother has something for us to do for her," Penny said. "She always wants us to gather the eggs and bring in kindling for the stove."

Mother packed a snack for Penny and Paul while they finished their chores.

"I'm glad Ula is too busy helping Mrs. Johnson to be in the

woods," Penny said. "I wouldn't trust her if we'd meet again and we were alone."

"I know you're right," he agreed.

The tall grass tickled the legs of the two hikers as they walked to the end of the lane. Huge trees shaded the forest floor. Birds chirped and flew from branch to branch. A gentle quietness filled the woods. Rays of sunlight slit through the trees.

"Dad says a deer trail is narrow and winds through the trees and brush," Paul shared.

"He also said to stay downwind so the deer won't smell us." Penny suggested. "Let's walk a straight line through the woods and we should be able to find a path if there is one. We don't know where the deer are yet so we don't have to worry about scaring them."

After Penny hunted through her part of the woods she called to Paul, "I haven't found anything. Nothing even begins to look like a trail. Have you found a path, Paul?"

"No, I don't see anything either," he called back. "Hey, what if it runs the other direction? We might have missed it. Let's try the other way."

"That's a good idea. I'll walk here and you go over toward the fence. We can cover a larger area," Penny motioned.

"Hey, I've found something," Paul waved.

Penny stopped, "You always find stuff. You can hardly be still for one minute and you are smarter than I am."

"Oh, come on Penny. Some things you know better." Paul smiled and pointed to the ground. "The grass is worn away and a thin path curves through the brush. Let's follow it and see if there is a tree to make a suitable fort in its branches."

"It's not a fort we want," Penny argued. "It's a tree house."

"No, it's not either one," Paul said. "We want to make a deer blind, remember? It's settled, okay?"

"Okay," Penny agreed.

35

"We need to find a tree with large leafy branches. A big one next to the trail so we can be over the path of the deer," Paul instructed.

Penny and Paul walked slowly, determined to find just the right place. "How's this one look?" Penny asked.

Paul studied the trail and the branches and settled the matter. "It looks about as perfect a tree as we'll be able to find. I'll climb up first and help you, Penny. Give me your hand. Good. We have a safe place to sit. Let's have our snack. I'm hungry," Paul rubbed his stomach.

Penny laughed, and said "We've only been gone a little while and you want to eat already. It does sound good though. Mom makes the best chocolate chip cookies."

"Shhh!" Paul put his finger to his mouth. "I hear something over there."

Penny looked where Paul pointed. The brush moved ever so slightly. A patch of white fur appeared.

Paul's heart beat hard. He thought it would scare their visitor away. He glanced at Penny and could tell by the look on her face that she saw it too. Silently they motioned to the same spot and nodded. The underbrush began to shake violently. Suddenly, the bushes parted and out burst Grandma's white German shepherd, old Prince.

After a stunned moment Paul whistled at the retreating white blur. Prince wheeled around and found his two friends in the tree. He ran to the tree, jumped, and lifted his paws up onto the trunk. His tongue hung out and he had a smile on his face.

"It looks like you've broken your chain again. We won't be able to see any deer with you around. I guess we'd better take you home," Paul sighed. "Whew! You sure gave us a scare."

CHAPTER 12
THE FAWN'S NAME

Grandma opened the door at Penny and Paul's knock. "Land sakes, where have you been off to, Princie? Aren't you the dearest kids to bring my dog home?" Grandma said.

Prince had exercised enough for the day and happily lay on the throw rug kept for him inside the kitchen.

After they told how they found Prince, Penny asked, "Would you call Mom and tell her we're on our way home?"

"Of course I will, but first you must have some milk and cookies." Grandma said.

She busied about the kitchen. Her long skirts almost touched the floor. Grandma wore her long gray hair pulled into a bun. With her cheeks rosy, blue eyes soft and smiling, she took some thin china from the cupboard and set the table for a snack.

"You must come and visit me more often," Grandma said.

"We'd love to, Grandma. We'll have more time with school out for the summer," Penny promised.

Paul put his hand on his chest. "Prince almost gave us a heart attack," he said. "I came close to falling out of the tree. We thought Prince was the albino fawn. He's about the same size and white. We'll try again to see our fawn. With a little luck we should find it."

Grandma answered, "I sure hope you do. It would be such a thrill. I don't think luck helps though. You should pray about it."

"Thank you for the cookies and milk," Penny said. "We'd better leave. It's time for us to go home and do our chores."

"I sure liked the snack. It tasted **more-ish**," Paul rubbed his stomach.

Grandma chuckled and picked up the phone and turned the crank on the side. "Hello, Central, give me the Harris place." While she waited she reminded them, "You must keep me up to date about your adventures. Oh, the operator is ringing now. I'll tell your mama you're on the way. Bye, bye, do come again soon."

After supper, Penny and Paul sat outside. "I'm glad we get off school earlier than the city kids," Paul said.

"Only because we're needed on the farm, and we don't get as many days off in the year either," Penny answered. "Our extra chores give Dad more time to work in the fields," Penny took a deep breath. "Everything smells fresh. Dad planted corn around the pond today."

Paul lay on the blanket Mother had given them to take outdoors. "Look how the leaves have grown on the brush and trees around the water. Even if the albino fawn is there, we couldn't see it there anymore."

"It's already too dark anyway," Penny said. "Look straight up, Paul. The stars look like thousands of diamonds on a black cloth."

Paul said, "I can find Venus and the Big Dipper. At the top

of the sky is the Little Dipper. I love this time of year. There are no mosquitoes and the snow has melted. There are billions of stars I can't begin to count them. The Bible tells us God stretched out his right hand and put every part of the universe in the heavens."

Penny answered, "It sure makes me feel small like a piece of dust or a tiny dot. He's more powerful and mighty than anyone or anything. Do you remember our Sunday school lesson, Paul? Who was the wisest person on earth?"

"You ask easy questions, Penny. It was Solomon. He followed God, never had war, and was the richest person ever. You should ask me how to track and find the white fawn. Why do you want to know about Solomon?"

Penny answered, "The Bible says Solomon in all his glory was not dressed as beautiful as the lilies of the field. I think our little fawn is as pretty as the trillium. If we find out it's a girl I'd like to name her Lily, 'Lily of the Field.'"

"Hey, that's neat," Paul said. "But if we find out it's a mighty stag we'd better call him 'Samson the Powerful,' named after the strongest person who ever lived."

"Agreed," answered Penny. "Anyway, it doesn't seem like we'll ever see the albino deer again. Every time we put potato peels by the trail they're gone when we check back. Probably raccoons have eaten them. We haven't seen one single deer yet. It seems like we'll never be at the same place at the same time as our deer."

"It's only the beginning of summer, Penny. We have plenty of time to watch for Samson."

"Lily," Penny smiled.

CHAPTER 13
RENEWED HOPE

"TODAY THE RASPBERRY PLANTS are full of white blossoms and red, juicy berries," Mother said. "I'd like you to help me make some jam today, Penny,"

Penny's mouth watered just thinking of the sweet berries. "What do you want me to do, Mom?"

"First wash those jars. We'll need them when the jam is ready to can. Put some water on the stove to boil. The jars will need to be sterilized."

Paul ran in from outside. "Mark is here and asked if I could go the woods with him today. May I, Mom?"

"Yes, but first we could use some help to pick the berries. Maybe Mark will help us and then he can take some home when he leaves. It'll be fun for all of us. Afterward, Penny and I will be busy making jam most of the morning. You mind yourself and don't get into trouble, and be back by noon."

"Sure Mom. I can't wait to eat some fresh jam."

"I wish I had your energy," Mom said. "We'll need at least

six quarts of berries. The bushes are picky with thorns. Be careful you don't get scratched."

Soon the fruit was picked and Paul and Mark left for the woods. A couple of hours later Penny and Mom admired their work.

"A job well done," Mom said. "Sample this jam. How does it taste?"

"Umm! Good!" Penny answered and took another bite.

Suddenly Paul burst into the kitchen. "Guess what happened to me?" He hollered.

"It must be something big by the grin on your face," Mom answered.

"Mark and I hid in the tree blind and lay really still. Mark nudged me to look at a deer that passed right under us. I moved over to get a better look. My sweatshirt fell and landed on its back. That doe gave a snort and carried my shirt down the trail."

Paul stopped to take a breath. "I saw her, Penny. I know it was our albino fawn. I saw her long enough to tell she's a Lily. Swish, she was gone in a white flash, can you believe it?"

"Oh, yes!" Penny's heart beat fast. "So the albino fawn is still here wonderful."

Her father's words echoed in her head: "Remember, honey, don't get your hopes up too high. You'll probably never see the fawn again." Still, she hoped he wasn't right and God's answer to her prayer to tame Lily would come true.

CHAPTER 14
MISTY'S BABIES

PENNY SAT QUIETLY ON the couch and watched Mother thread a needle with blue thread. She tied a knot in the end and continued to mend the knee of Paul's jeans. "Honestly Penny, your brother tears more holes in his blue jeans. I tell him not to slide on the back porch cement. If he doesn't tear holes in his pants he gets grass stains on his shirts." Mom shook her head. "Paul doesn't worry about his clothes."

Penny yawned and Mom glanced her way. "What's the matter honey? Are you tired?"

"No, I guess not. I'm bored," Penny answered.

Mother nodded. "You know the solution, young lady. I can always find some job for you to do."

"I know," Penny said. "Dad and Paul have gone fishing, and I'd like something fun to do."

Mom agreed, "I feel like skipping work and just enjoying something different in my life. Everyday chores get dull, but they need to be done anyway."

Mom thought and worked with the thread. "Why don't you go to the barn and look for Misty? Dad said she should have her kittens any day now. She didn't drink milk with the other cats this morning."

"Oh yes, I'll go to the barn and look for them." replied Penny, and headed for the back door.

"Wait," called Mom. "If you find her and she has her litter, be very careful not to scare her. She hasn't been with us long and she might move her family away."

Penny answered, "Don't worry, Mom. Misty has been here about four months hasn't she? She was so skinny and ran away from all of us. You told Paul and me to put leftover food in an old pie tin, and leave it on the porch. Remember how we'd wait for her to sneak from the cornfield and creep to the supper scraps? Paul sat like a statue on the porch while Misty made her way to the dish, and one day she let Paul reach out his hand and pet her. She's been our favorite cat. I like her name too. Her color reminds me of the foggy mist that rises off our pond in the morning. Bye, Mom, I'm heading for the barn."

Penny opened the barn door. "Here, kitty, kitty, kitty." She called softly. She walked to the back of the barn and listened. The gentle breeze made soft noises near the roof. Sparrows chirped and flew from their nests to hunt insects. Rays of light drifted between gray wooden slats of the wall. Penny held her breath so she could hear better. "*I love this old barn,*" she thought. "*All its smells and noises.*" She strained to listen for a meow.

"No, there is nothing here. I know I'll climb the ladder above the cow stanchions. Maybe Misty made a place to have her kittens near the straw bales." The floor held some broken furniture, old tool parts, and clean bedding for the cattle.

Penny called softly for Misty so as not to scare her. "Kitty, kitty, kitty." Upon hearing a faint meow, she called a little louder, "Kitty, kitty." She moved toward the sound.

Thump! Something landed behind her. Penny jumped. "Oh, Misty, it's you." She held her chest and laughed.

"Meow." The gentle cat purred and walked back and forth under Penny's hand.

"You're so skinny, Misty. It looks like you've had your babies. Where are those little sweethearts?"

She stroked Misty's fur. "Let's find your kitties." Penny climbed across the straw to the direction the mother cat had jumped. Next to the barn wall was a small, round hole, and inside she could see fur.

Misty was at her side and didn't mind her looking. Instead, it seemed she was happy and proud to show off her new family. Misty crawled into the round smooth hole next to her kittens.

Penny watched. "I see three," she counted. "Oh, how cute and little they are. Their eyes are tightly shut, but they know their mother's here. They're so tiny, look at them search to find their dinner. Let me see. One is white with a black spot near its left ear. This one is a gray tiger, like you, Misty, and the third one is a calico color. You take care of your babies just like Lily's mother takes care of Lily."

Penny lightly stroked the fur with her finger. She did not pick them up even though she wanted to hold them. They are just too little. "I'd better wait a few days," she whispered.

"Oh, Misty, I think you're hungry. I'll get something for you right away." Penny felt guilty about not thinking of the new mother sooner.

"Penny," someone called from the barn floor.

CHAPTER 15
ULA AGAIN

CHILLS WENT DOWN PENNY's spine. "Oh no, look who it is—Ula!" Penny stumbled backward to hide. She felt cornered.

"There you are, Penny," Ula said and climbed the ladder. Ula saw the fear on Penny's face. "Don't be afraid," she spoke softly. "So much has happened to me since I saw you and Paul in the woods. Mrs. Johnson is here to visit your mom."

Penny glanced around. "This is probably a trick. She's going to push me off. I'll inch toward the ladder so I can escape," she softly said.

"Let's sit on these bales of straw. I want to tell you all about it." Ula motioned.

"You sit on the bale, Ula. I'll pull up this crate." Penny made sure she was near the ladder.

Ula chattered on and didn't seem to notice Penny's plan. "It was when Paul said God and Jesus loved me when we met in the woods. Remember?"

"Uh, sure, I remember, Ula. Paul and I had to go back

to our house because Dad blew the car horn," Penny forced herself to answer.

"I'm excited," continued Ula. "Part of the agreement to work for the Johnsons was I'd go to church with them. I rebelled at first. I hated it. I thought everyone would hate me. I only agreed to work for them because my family needed the money. I could help my family with what I could earn."

Penny thought to herself, *she doesn't act mean and she's being nice to me. I still don't trust her, and I'm not going to tell her about Misty's babies.*

Penny started to listen to Ula again.

"Pastor Leonard said the same thing Paul did and more. He said Jesus loved me so much He gave His life for my sin. Pastor bowed his head and prayed this prayer: 'I feel there is someone who Jesus is calling to come to Him.'"

"I knew he was talking to me. All I had to do was ask Jesus to forgive my sin and come into my heart. I walked down the aisle and stood in the front of the church. I knelt and asked Jesus to be my Lord. Mrs. Johnson cried and told me, 'These are tears of joy.' It was the happiest day of my life."

Penny stood up and opened her arms to Ula. Her eyes stung. "I was afraid of you, but I can see you have changed."

The girls sat on the bales of straw and talked. Penny told Ula all about King Solomon and the lilies and how she named the albino fawn "Lily of the Field."

"I know what I saw wasn't a ghost or a spirit," Ula said. "The hoot I heard must have been an owl. My folks tell fortunes and always talk about spirits, but I know this is wrong. I pray for my dad and mom. I love my parents. Pastor Leonard told me I was calling for the devil or a demon to come. He said God must have sent you and Paul there at the right time. I'm so glad you were in the woods. I hope you and Paul get to tame your little deer. Listen, I hear Sarah Johnson calling me. It's time to go. I'll see you later, Penny. Bye." Then Ula laughed and acted as if she would push Penny off the loft.

Penny called after her. "That wasn't funny, Ula."

Back at the house, Penny told Mother how Ula pretended like she was going to push Penny down.

Mom answered. "We've been given good news about Ula, but don't expect her to change right away. Ula is like a baby now; she has a lot to learn about Jesus. Babies need everything done for them. You have to feed them, change their clothes, carry them, and teach them all about growing up. Most people who ask Jesus into their heart won't seem much different right away. I'm glad she is a Christian now. The Lord will work on her heart. It takes time, sometimes it takes a long time. Let's pray Ula is a fast learner."

CHAPTER 16
TWO NEW FRIENDS

THE THERMOMETER ON THE oak tree next to the back porch read ninety-four degrees on the twenty-eighth of July.

A tan jeep with two men drove up the Harris driveway.

Dad and the family sat on the porch and enjoyed the cool shade.

The men waved a friendly greeting. "Hello, we've been given as assignment by the game warden. I'm Officer Fred Reed and this is Officer Al Brandon."

"Hello," Dad greeted. "Come on up and have some lemonade with us. Anything we can do for you men?"

"Thank you. A cold drink sounds mighty good." Al and Fred shook hands with everyone. "We're here to check on the wild turkey. We've heard some might be back in this area. We're looking for people to let us do some research on their land. We'd like to count the birds, if there are any."

Dad scratched his head and thought through this information. "It's all right with me if you fellows do some work here.

I have two woods on my property and I can tell you we don't have any turkeys in the one to the east. Probably your best place to work would be over in the north woods. We don't go there often and the turkeys would have a safer place to nest."

"You may set up camp there if you'd like to." Dad offered.

Paul broke in excitedly, "We often hear bobwhites in the evening. Some whippoorwills are around here too." Paul whistled the calls.

"Hey, pretty good," Officer Bob commented with a touch of mischief in his voice. "I can't call anything with a whistle. I need to put salt on their tail as my old Pappy used to say. My lips can pucker and I can blow but nothing comes out but a wet spray. It's a burden not being able to whistle."

Dad laughed and changed the subject. "Does either of you have any unusual stories in your line of work?"

Both of the men broke out in laughter. "Funny you should ask," Al chuckled. "Last fall before hunting season we were north of here. Our job was to check on reported deer poaching. It was September. We'd had an early snow and were looking for tracks."

Fred took over the story. "I sent Al to the right and I went to the left in the forest."

Al cut in. "We had been given a tranquilizer gun in case we came across any buck deer. The gun was something we don't usually have. We were using it as an experiment for the department. The gun had recently been invented to shoot a dart to tranquilize animals that need attention or catching. During the autumn season male deer have been known to be aggressive and even dangerous."

Fred explained, "One of our officers was gored by a buck in the same area last year. He made it to the car and blew the horn until his partner came."

"Was he all right?" Mom asked.

"After a trip to the hospital and some rest he recovered,"

Fred answered. "But that's not the story. We both were looking for footprints or other clues to help us."

Al continued. "I jumped over a log right onto the back of an old black bear! I don't know who was more scared, me or mister black bear! I think it was me because he gave one loud growl and ran after me."

Fred smiled. "Yeah, here came Al moving faster than I ever saw him move and yelling louder than I ever heard him yell. 'Help! Help! Help!' I saw the bear then grabbed the tranquilizer gun and aimed. I hit him with the first shot. He was one loud, mean furball…"

"Did it stop him?' Dad asked.

"We didn't wait to see. The gun was loaded for deer a little over two hundred pounds," Al answered. "This bear probably weighed between three hundred fifty to four hundred pounds and he was ugly. I saw Fred and yelled, "Run to the jeep." We ran as far and fast as we could until I ran out of breath and had a pain in my side."

"We looked behind us for the bear. The dart must have slowed him down enough to give us time to get away." Al took a deep breath. "Oowee!" He hollered. "We've never had a more wild and dangerous adventure."

By this time everyone laughed and marveled at the two men's story.

"It's a good thing we don't have bears around here," Dad added.

"Al insists on us carrying that tranquilizer gun," Fred said.

"I don't see you complain any," Al answered.

The men agreed they'd be back early the next day to set up camp on the farm.

"By the way," Dad said, "this spring we spotted an albino fawn down by the pond. Maybe you could keep an eye out for it."

"We'll sure try. Albino deer are a rare find and we would treasure a sight of it." Fred tipped his hat. "It's time to go and we'll see you tomorrow. Thanks for the drink."

CHAPTER 17
THE ENCOUNTER

A SOFT SCENT OF flowers filled the unusually cool August day. Penny picked a small bouquet of deep red roses from the garden, and walked to the house.

Mother looked up as her daughter entered. "Those blossoms are lovely, honey," she said. "Just smell the fragrance. Get a jar and put them into water."

Penny took a milk glass vase and arranged the flowers.

"Oh my!" gasped Mother and she covered her mouth with her hand. "It's past time to send a snack to the field. I didn't watch the time as I should have. Dad and Paul will be ready for a few cookies and a drink."

Penny nodded. "Dad and Paul are always ready for something to eat or drink."

"I can't disagree. Those two have empty stomachs most of the time." smiled Mom.

"A canning jar will be good to use for some fresh cool water from the pump, and take a few of these chocolate chip

51

cookies. I know they're looking for you to bring them a snack. They'll stop working and take their break."

"Mom, may I wear Paul's old red sweatshirt?" Penny asked. "I'm sure he wouldn't mind. It has hung here most of the summer."

"Yes, go ahead, honey. Dad and Paul are out in the east field by the woods to check and mend the fence."

The two workers were pleased with their treat and stopped gladly to rest a while. Penny had cookies too. Later she left for the north woods, after asking her father's permission.

Penny came to her favorite spot. She began to pretend she was an Indian girl. *History of the area tells us members of the Ottowa tribe used to hunt on our land,* Penny remembered. *Dad finds arrowheads when he plows. More proof other people were here earlier. They must have walked through the ferns like I'm doing. Maybe an Indian girl picked wildflowers for her hair too just like I'm doing now.*

She walked into a meadow near their creek. A tree trunk had fallen into the water, and the larger end remained on land. Penny crept to the end of the log. She was careful not to fall.

Plunk, plunk—a couple of ever-present green and black frogs jumped into the water. Penny peeked over the edge of the trunk. "I don't look like an Indian girl with my blonde hair and yellow eyes, but she could have seen her reflection the same way I'm seeing mine." She whispered. Peering deep into the water she could see plants growing from the bottom. Tiny silver minnows darted around the protective stems and leaves.

Suddenly, out of the corner of her eye, she spied a shape. *What's behind me?* She thought. Her body began to shake. Slowly she raised her head and turned around to look.

The albino fawn stood, sniffed the air, and took a step toward Penny.

Penny inched off the log onto a patch of grass. Ever so slowly, the fawn stepped toward her stiff-legged as if she was pushed.

"My Lily, oh, my sweet Lily," Penny's heart was beating fast. She quietly spoke as the young albino doe came nearer little by little.

"How soft and large your eyes are. Your fur is like a princess's coat. You're beautiful," Penny whispered.

The delicate light ears moved back and forth. Again the fawn moved closer. Her nostrils twitched as she smelled Penny's scent.

Penny stretched her arm to touch Lily's pale nose. Lily jumped and slowly moved back into the underbrush.

For a moment, Penny was too stunned to move. "Oh, but I must go and tell Dad and Paul right away."

CHAPTER 18
DANGEROUS SITUATION

Dad stepped back from the fence and gave his forehead a wipe with his sleeve. "Whew, this fence post shouldn't break for a long time," he said.

Paul looked up and saw Penny. She shouted and ran toward them.

"What's the ruckus about, Punkus?" Dad teased with his pet name for her.

Penny, excited, told her story. "It's the truth. It really is," she said. "I can hardly believe it myself."

"Deer just don't come up to people," Paul said. "Why would our fawn walk up to you and let you touch her? Dad says they're too wild and its mother would protect it."

"Wait a minute, Son," Dad said gently, and put his hand on Paul's shoulder. "You and Mark saw Lily's mother in the woods. Didn't you say you dropped your red sweatshirt on her? Lily was there too, wasn't she?"

"Yes, my sweatshirt fell on the doe and the fawn was there."

"Penny is wearing your red sweatshirt. Our Lily smelled the scent of her mother on your sweatshirt. Things don't sound right though. We'd better go take a look."

They arrived at the pond and Dad studied the area. "Which direction did the fawn disappear into the woods after it jumped away from you, Penny?"

"Over there," she pointed to a grove of maple trees.

"You two follow along behind me like Indians with moccasins on their feet … real quiet." Dad instructed.

They walked a short distance into the woods. Dad held up his hand. "I hear a thumping noise ahead," he whispered. "I'm going to lift you two onto a tree limb over there," Dad said. "If what I hear is a wounded animal it'll be dangerous." The wind is blowing toward us so our scent shouldn't give us away."

It was hard for Penny and Paul to stay quiet in the tree and not know what Dad would find.

Soon he came back. "Over the hill, Lily's mother is caught in an old fence row. She's got some wire twisted around her body and a couple of posts across her back. I know she is our little fawn's mother because the Lily is by her side."

Penny's voice shook as she asked, "What can we do? Can we free her, Dad?"

"She won't die if we work quickly, but I don't dare walk up to her. She's frightened and she might hurt herself," Dad answered. "Paul, run as fast as you can to Fred and Al's camp. They'll know how to handle this. If you're not back soon enough for her to be safe, I'll try the wire cutters to get her loose … but, I'd rather not try this alone."

Paul knew he was fast. He was proud Dad had given him the job. He ran swiftly and easily missed trees and rocks.

Paul quickly reached the camp but no one could be seen.

He cupped his hands to his mouth and yelled, "Fred, Al, Help!"

Before the last word left his lips, Fred appeared. "What's the matter, Paul? It sounds like an emergency."

"It is," said Paul, and hurriedly told them the problem.

Fred took out a whistle and blew three short, three long, and three short blasts. He turned to Paul. "We use the SOS signal."

Al came right away. Fred packed their bag with speed, and Al grabbed the tranquilizer gun. "We can calm the doe so we can rescue her and she won't hurt us either," Fred stated.

"Come on. We've no time to waste. Paul, you lead the way. We'll follow as fast as we can," Fred said.

CHAPTER 19
RESCUED

DAD SAT ON THE ground under the tree where Penny waited. A breeze rippled through the branches and sent a shiver through her body. "How long has Paul been gone, Dad?" Penny asked.

Dad pulled his pocket watch out of his overalls. "About twenty minutes, honey."

Penny couldn't remember when time had passed so slowly. She wanted to climb down and run to the trapped doe. She knew Dad would do everything he could, but what about her precious Lily?

Another minute passed and Penny leaned over the limb. "Hey, Dad, I can see Paul with Fred and Al."

The two officers agreed they would tranquilize the doe. "We'll have to work at a fast pace to loosen the posts around her and remove the barbed wire," Fred said.

"Paul and I have our wire cutters," Dad offered. "You and Al can push over the old fence. It doesn't look solid. The wire is twisted around the doe's neck and legs. Paul will help me cut the barbed wire loose."

The small band of people watched as Fred crept up the hill and took aim. The shot found its mark and soon after the doe slumped into a relaxed position.

Fred stood tall and waved for everyone to follow him.

Fred and Al pulled and tugged the posts. They were rotten from being in the ground a long time. It didn't take long to snap and remove the old wood. Working fast, Dad and Paul clipped and cut the wire from the doe's body.

Penny stood near Lily and soothed her. "Don't worry, Lily. We won't hurt your mother. We're trying to help her get free. In no time at all you'll be able to run next to her like you always have."

Lily seemed to understand and stepped closer to Penny.

"Deer sometimes get so tangled in old fence rows they starve to death or die from fright." Fred said. "It's a good thing you found her when you did. She looks all right. I'll put salve on her leg. It's scratched. Nothing is broken. She'll be okay. The fawn's mother hasn't been caught long."

Al took some pictures with his box camera. "I can't understand why the fawn doesn't run away. She's standing so close to Penny, pretty as a picture. Look at her pink nose, ears, and eyes. Lily is the Miss America of the forest."

"Yes, she is," Fred said. "Okay, we're done. The deer is free. Let's all hurry to the top of the hill and hide. There's plenty of cover and we'll be out of sight and won't scare the doe while the drug wears off. Be sure to sit still and don't make any noise."

All five people were hidden in the brush when Lily's mother began to move. First her head rose and fell back. She struggled to stand on her feet. In a dazed state she snorted, and the albino jumped to her side. The two sniffed each other and slowly walked into the woods.

"It's a thrill to be able to save one of God's creatures," Fred said softly.

Al nodded and cleared his throat. "We'll clear this wire out of here so nothing else gets caught."

Dad extended his hand to Al and Fred. "We don't quite know how to thank you men."

"You don't have to," Fred replied and took Dad's hand. "It is all part of our job and this has been a pleasure."

On the way home Paul whooped and laughed. "I can't wait for school to start."

"What?" Penny asked in disbelief. "I never heard you wish for school to start."

"Teachers always ask us to write about our summer vacation. I'll have a great story. With pictures too, because Al promised he'd bring us some," Paul said.

Dad and Paul talked excitedly on the way back to the house and could hardly wait to share the news with Mom.

Penny fell a couple steps behind them. *Wasn't it lucky?* She thought. *Mother was late with the snacks. Dad and Paul had their wire cutters because they were working on the fence. Of course Fred and Al just happened to be in the woods.*

The truth of it all rushed through her. She took a quick glance on all sides for her guardian angel but saw only bright sunshine. Grandma said luck has nothing to do with it. "I know Jesus, you used all of these things to save my Lily," Penny prayed.

"One thing is for sure," she continued, as a tear rolled down her cheek. "I'll never ever forget today. Thank you, God. You answered my prayers. You saved my precious Lily, my own lily of the field."

Synopsis

PENNY AND PAUL HARRIS see a mysterious object in their fields at dusk. It seems to hop around and appears and disappears from their sight.

Ula, an older girl at school, tells them they have seen an evil spirit or a ghost and that Penny and Paul will have bad luck. Ula is bent on causing them trouble.

School is out, and the Harris children have the summer to search for answers and follow their hearts.

From Bible stories they learn that Jesus has promised to guide them and will always hear their prayers.

About the Author:

FRANCES J HARIG LIVES in southern Michigan with her husband, Richard. She is a child of God, a wife, a mother, a grandmother, and a great grandmother. Her greatest joy is telling others about Jesus. She and her husband attend Parkside Bible Church in Holland, Michigan. Besides writing for children, she loves to draw and paint.

LaVergne, TN USA
31 December 2009
168614LV00001B/4/P